YOU'RE AMAZING!

Wonder Woman created by William Moulton Marston

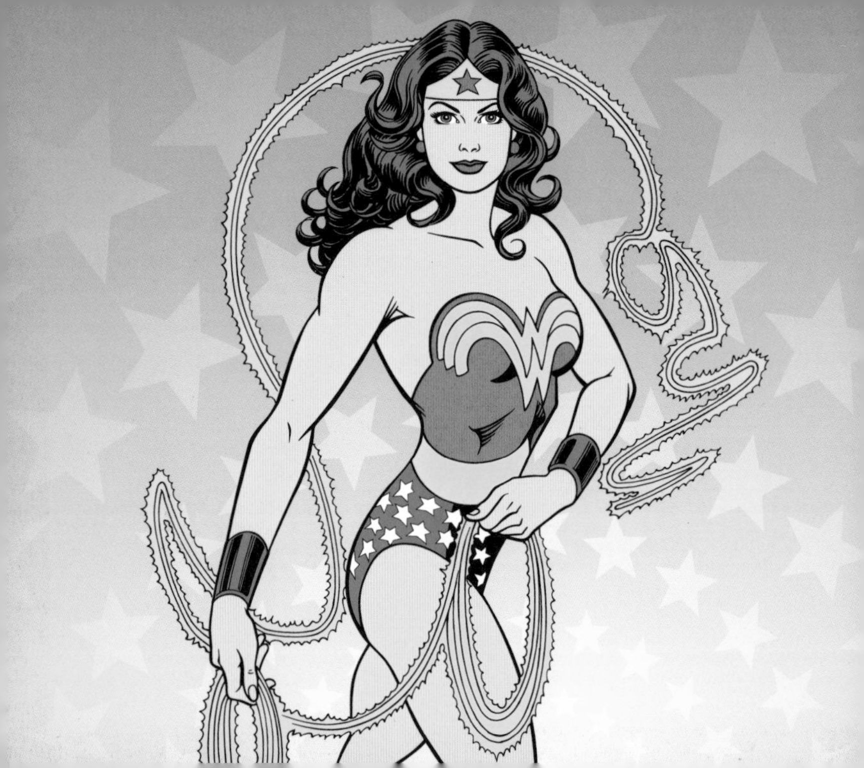

I admire the way you always fight for

_____ .

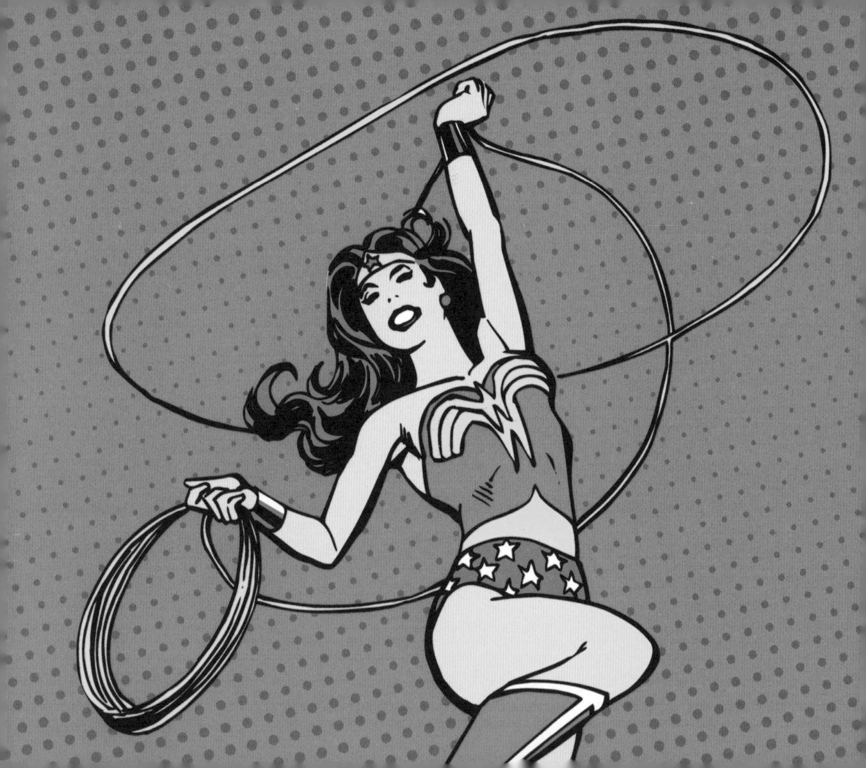

Your superpower is

_____ .

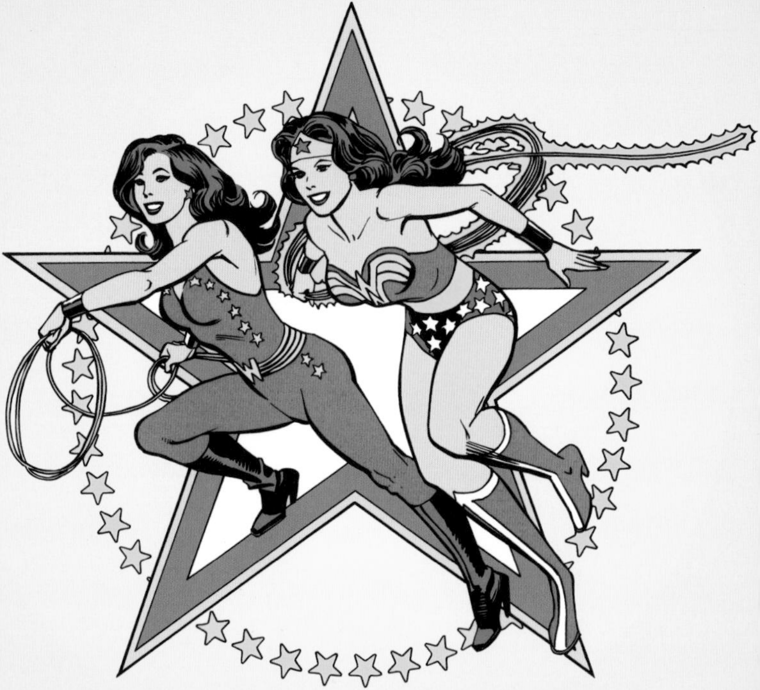

You taught me that sisterhood

_____ .

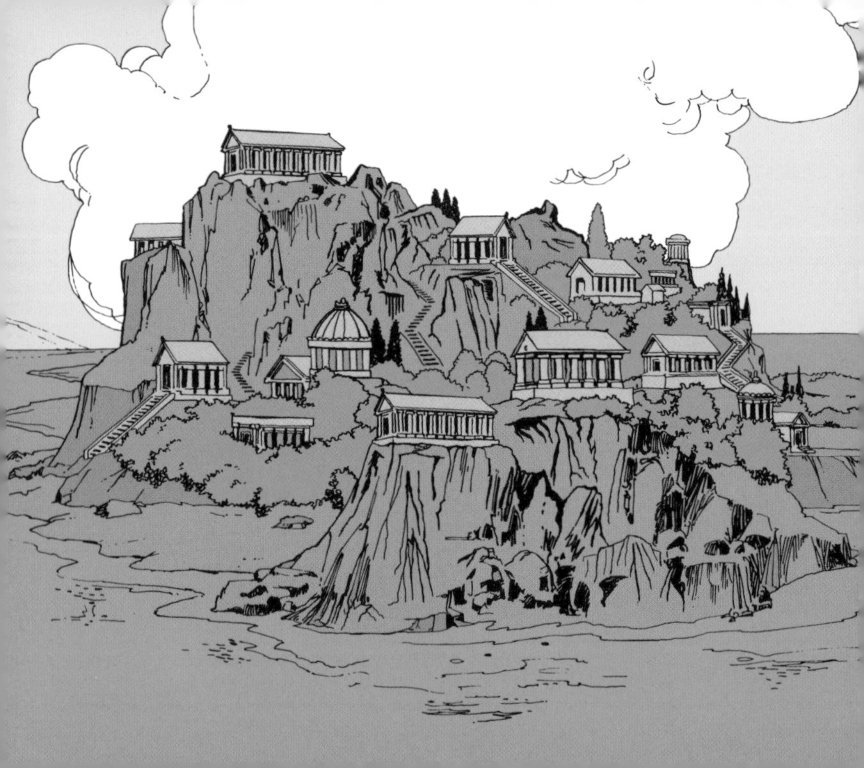

You make your home as welcoming
as Paradise Island by

_____ .

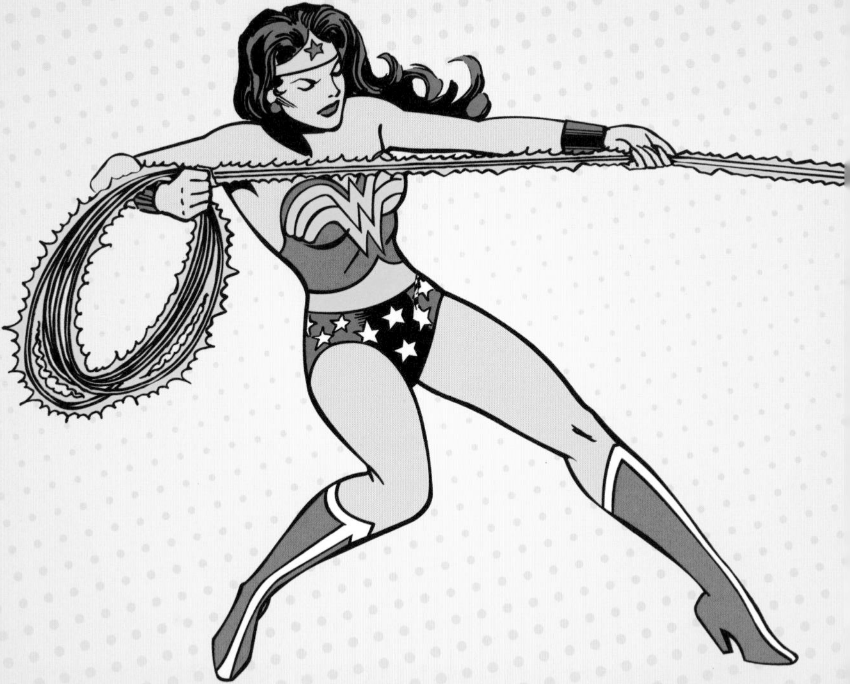

I can't help but tell you
the truth when you

_____ .

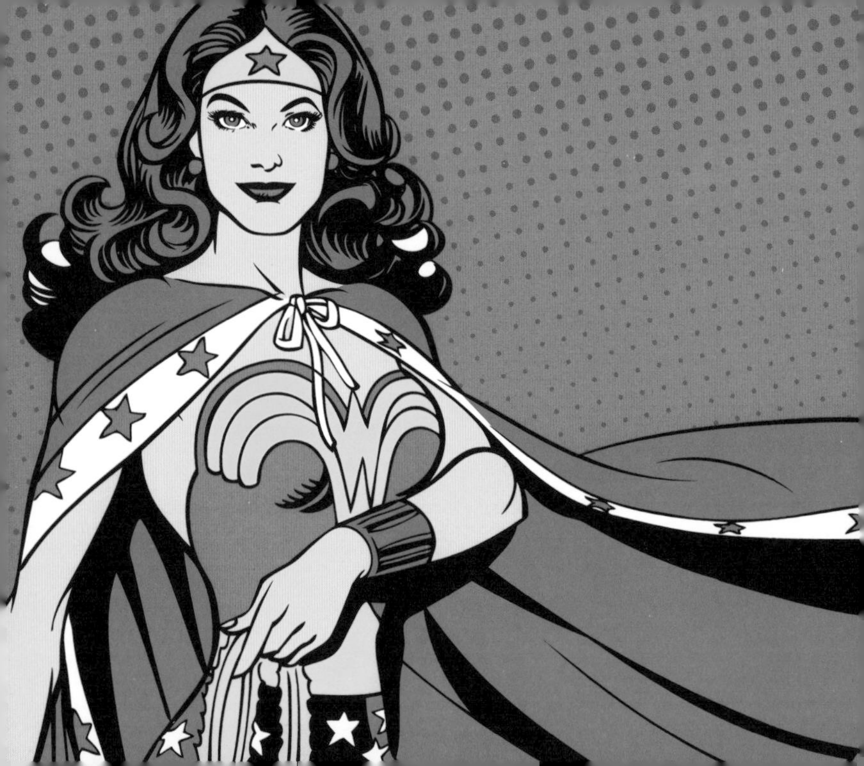

You’re such a princess when you

______________________________ .

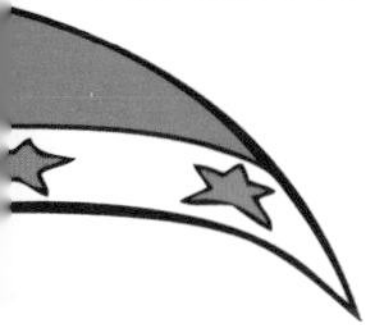

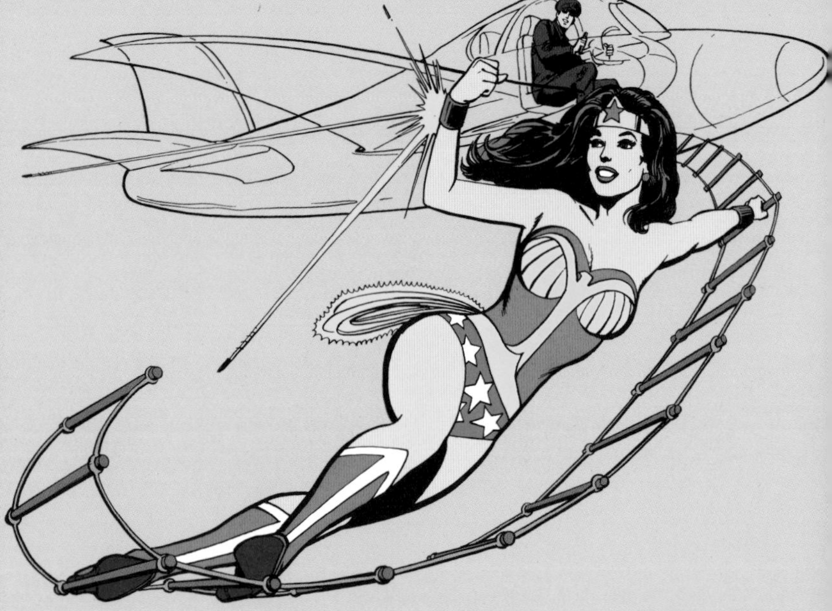

Your ability to

_____

must have come from
Hippolyta herself!

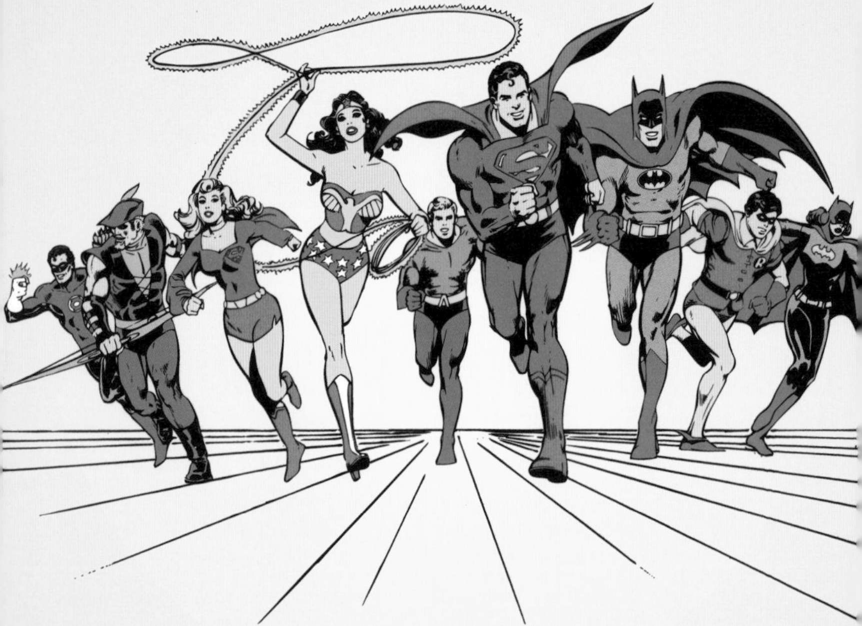

We made a superpowered
team when we

_____ .

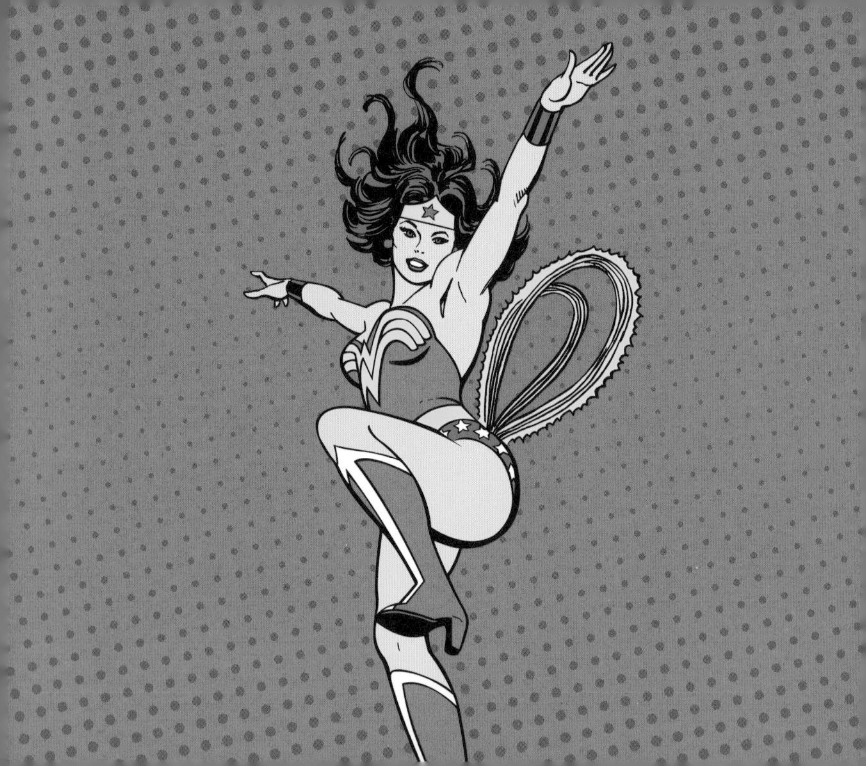

I feel safe when you

_____ .

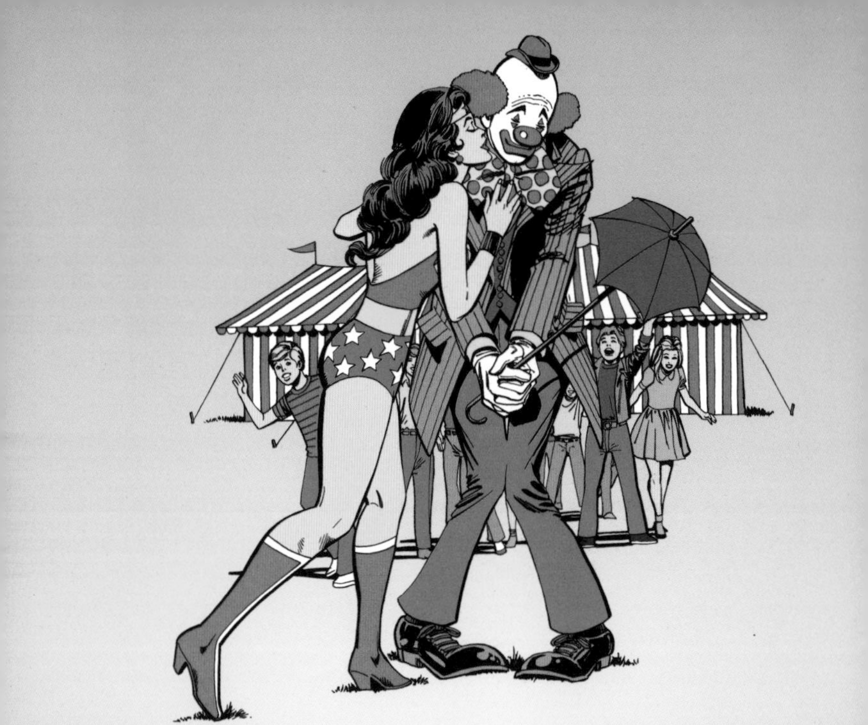

Your capacity to love is
rivaled only by your

_____ .

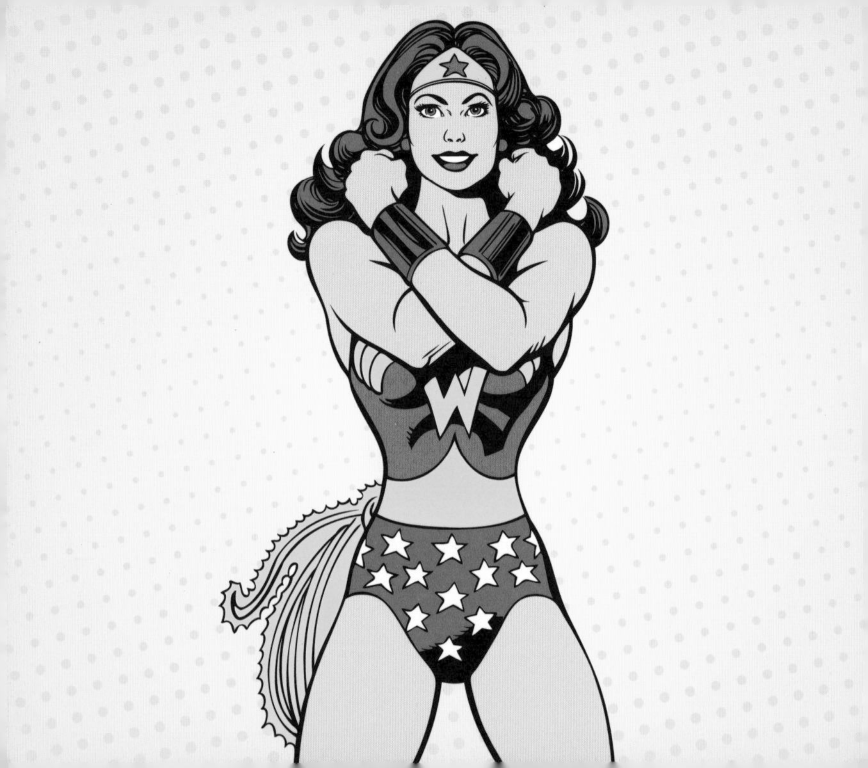

Of all your accessories,
I love the way you rock your

_____

the most.

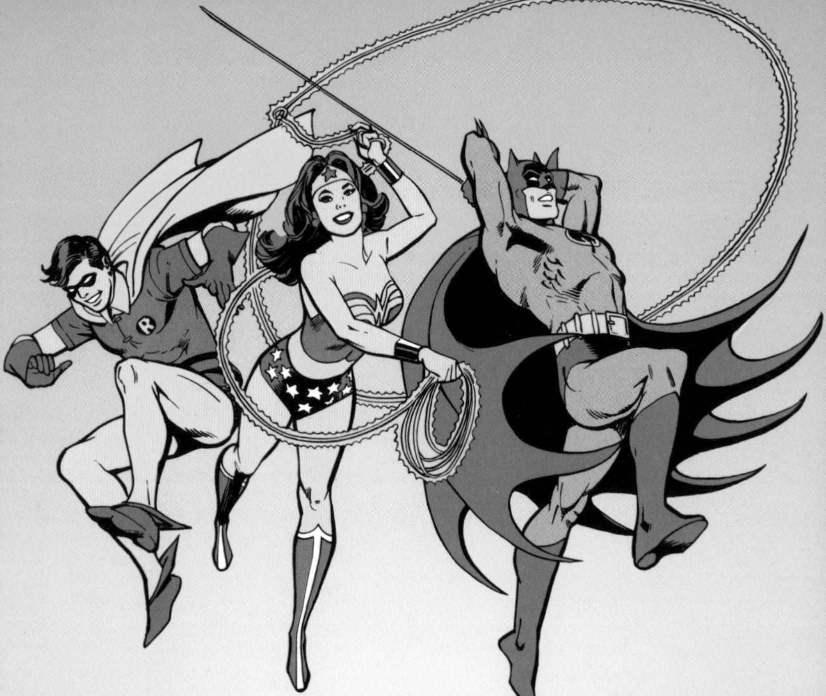

Your bracelets may not
stop bullets, but your

_____

stops

_____ .

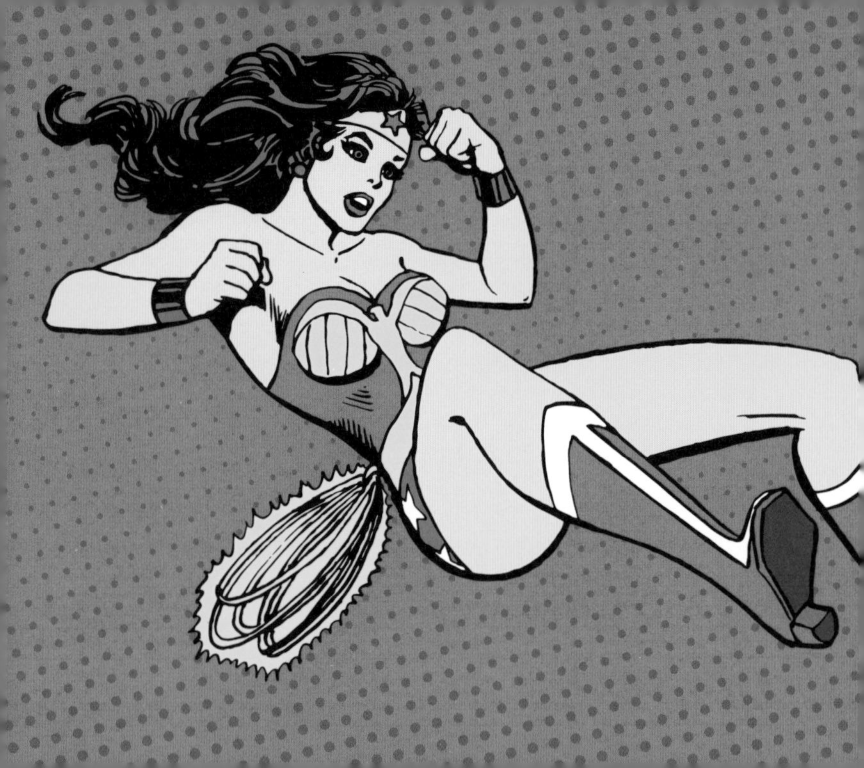

Your

is so sharp it cuts

down to size.

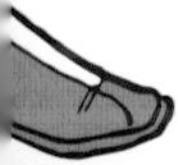

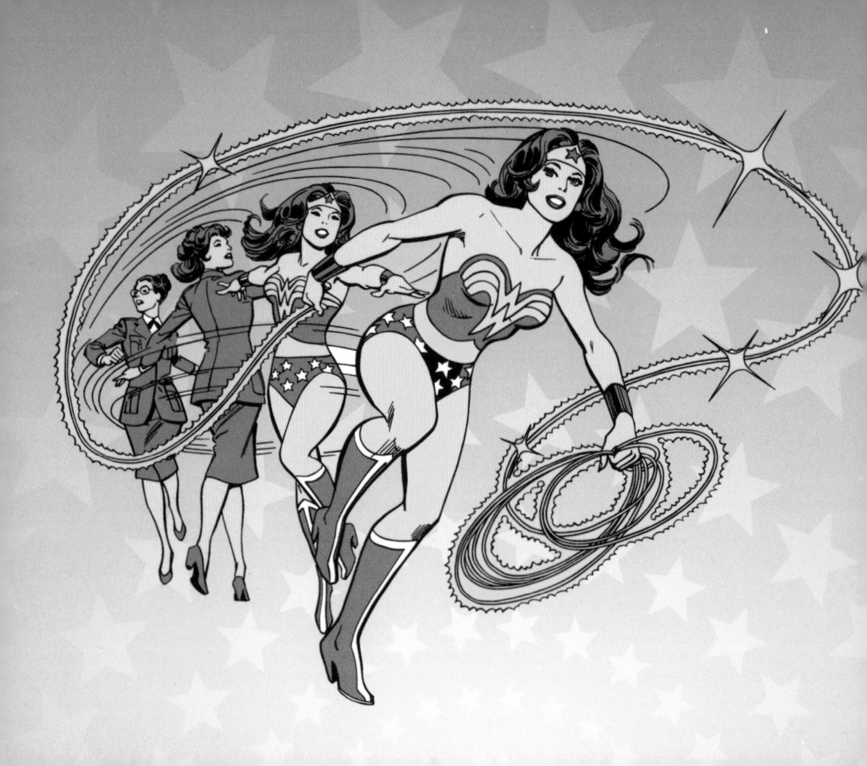

You taught me that you don't have to spin in circles to change

_____ .

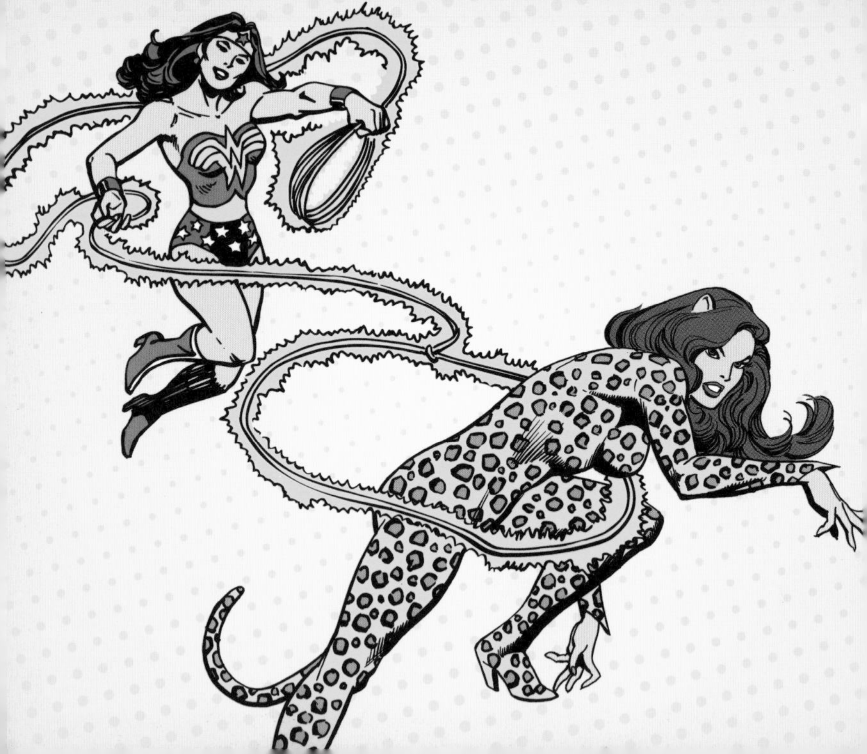

Your arch nemesis can never defeat your

_____ .

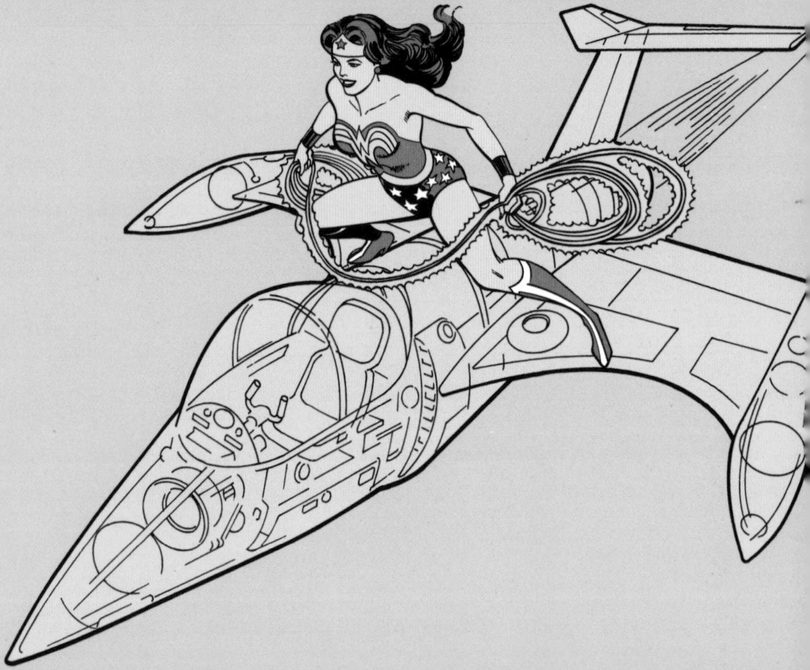

Your

_____

may not be practical
but you look amazing in it!

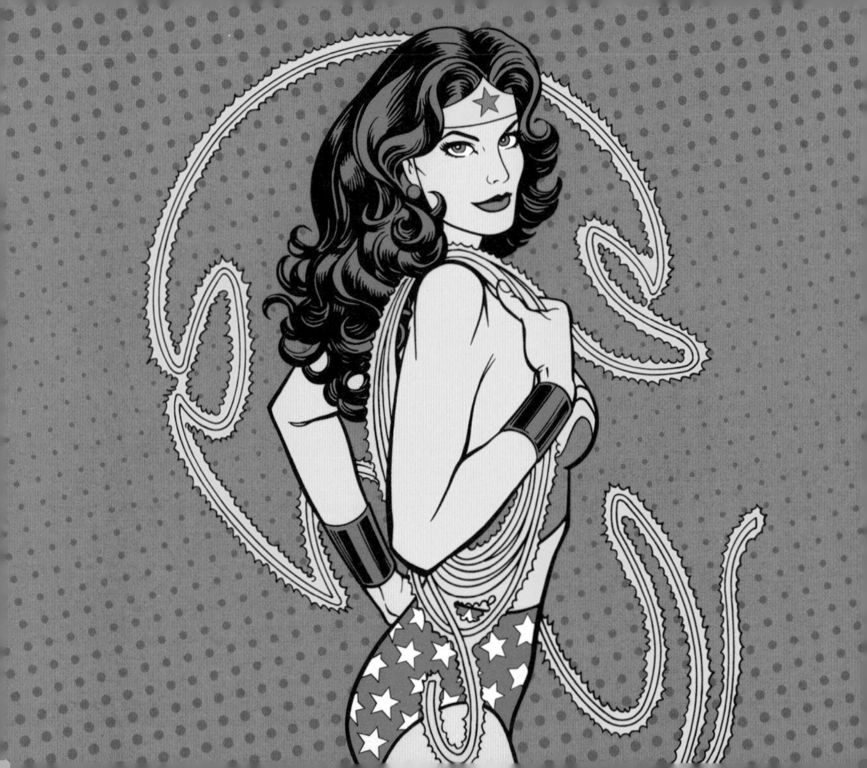

You honor the women who
came before you by

_____ .

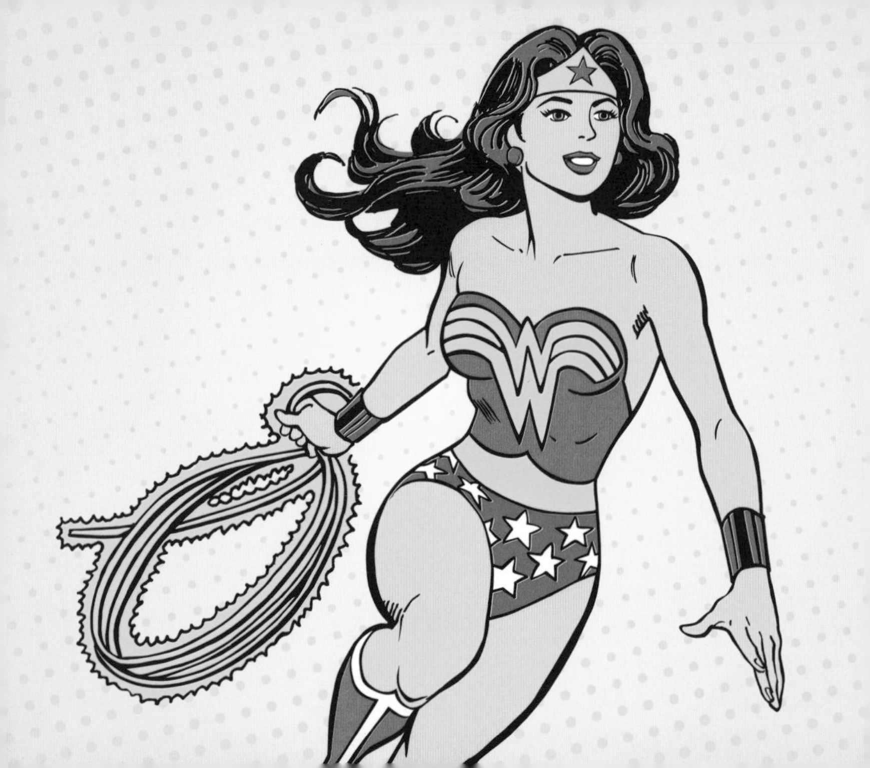

Ares could never defeat you because

_____ .

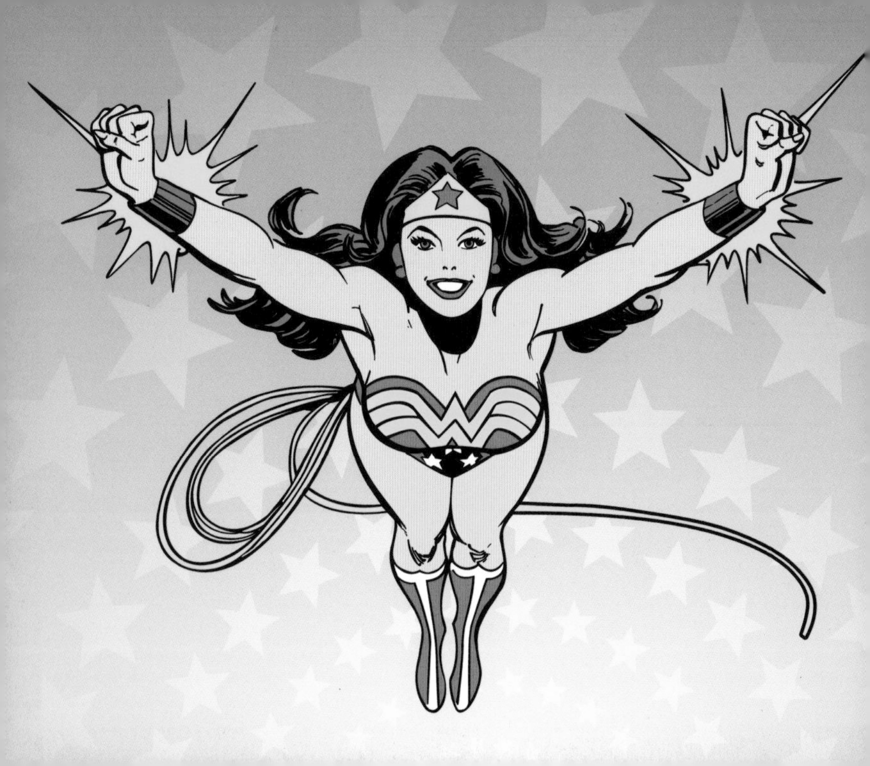

You're my hero because

_____ .

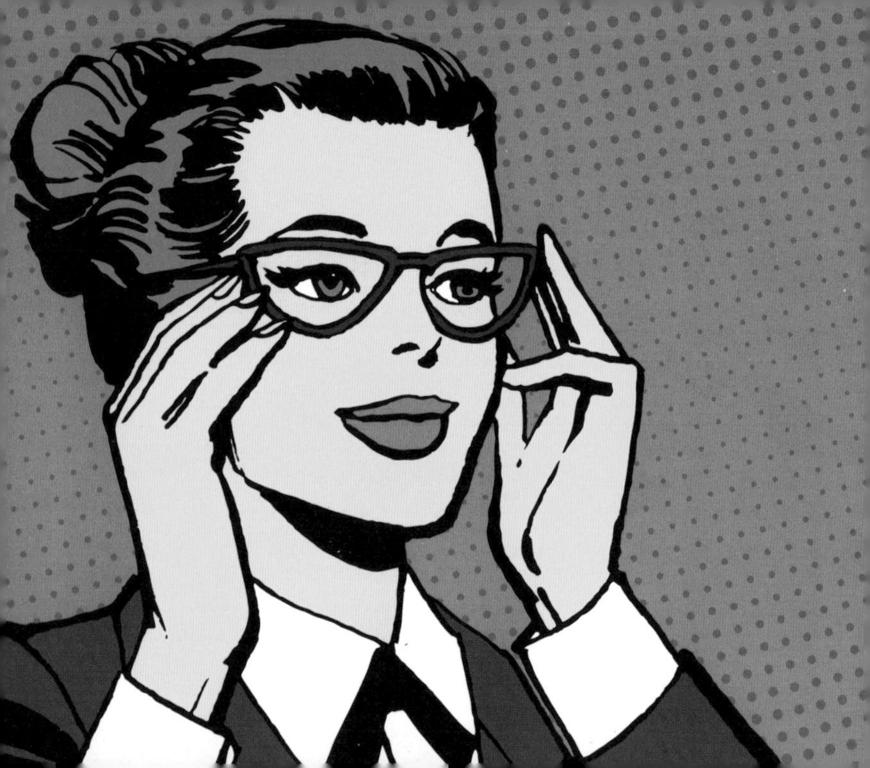

Your secret identity as a

_____

is safe with me!

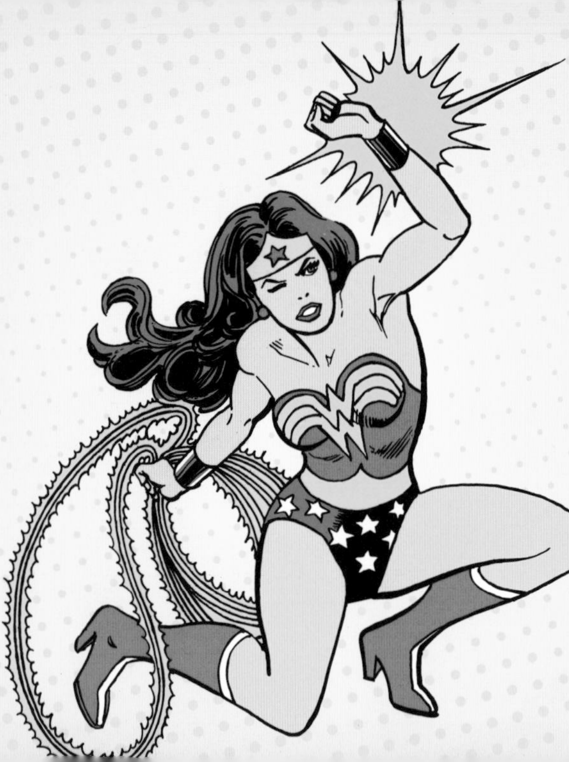

You're strong enough to

_____ ,

but gentle enough to

_____ .

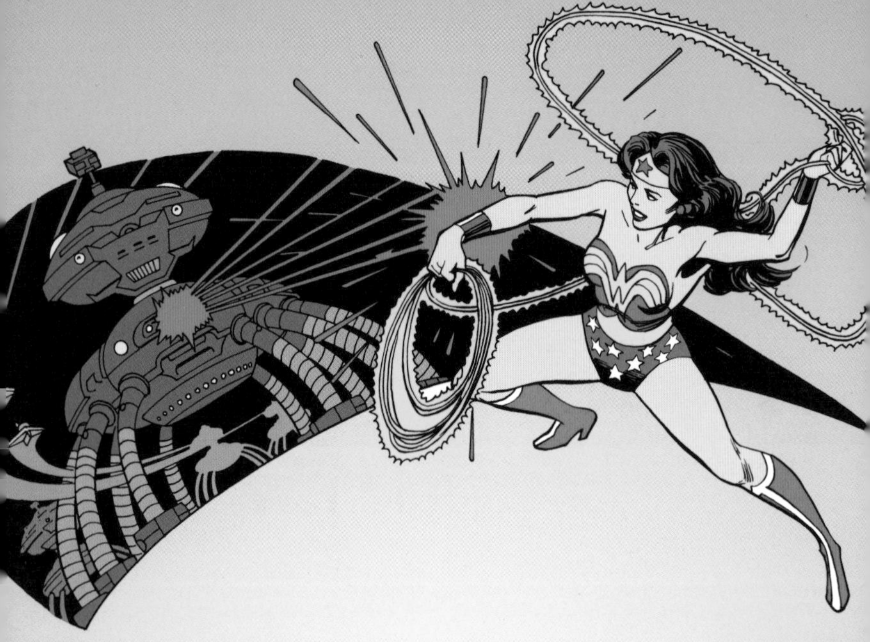

You protect everyone from

_____ .

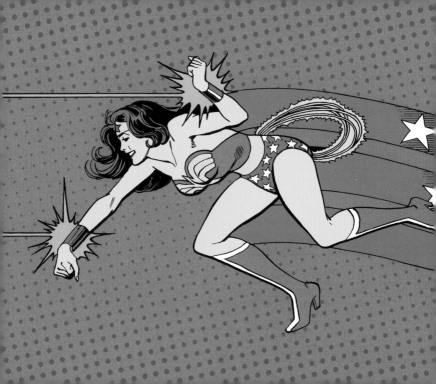

I wonder how you're able to

_____ .

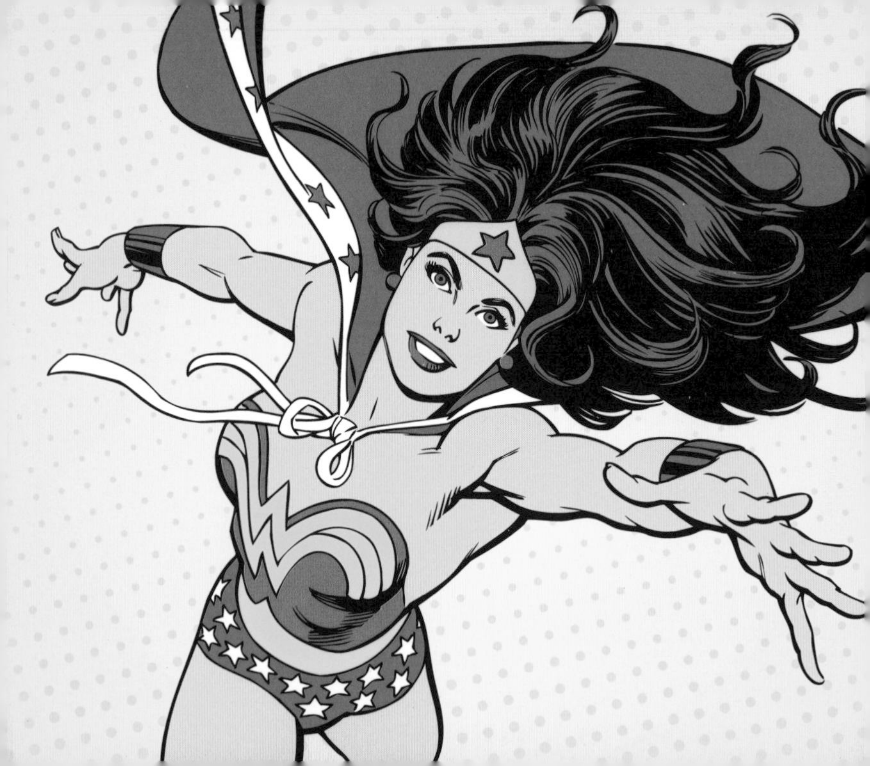

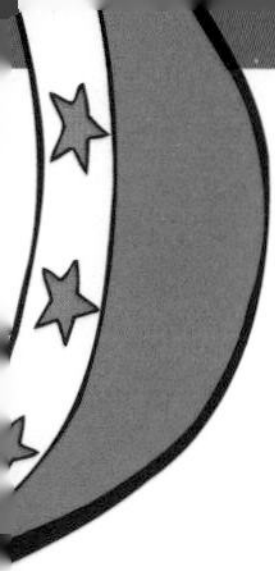

Your mission of

____

is an inspiration to us all.

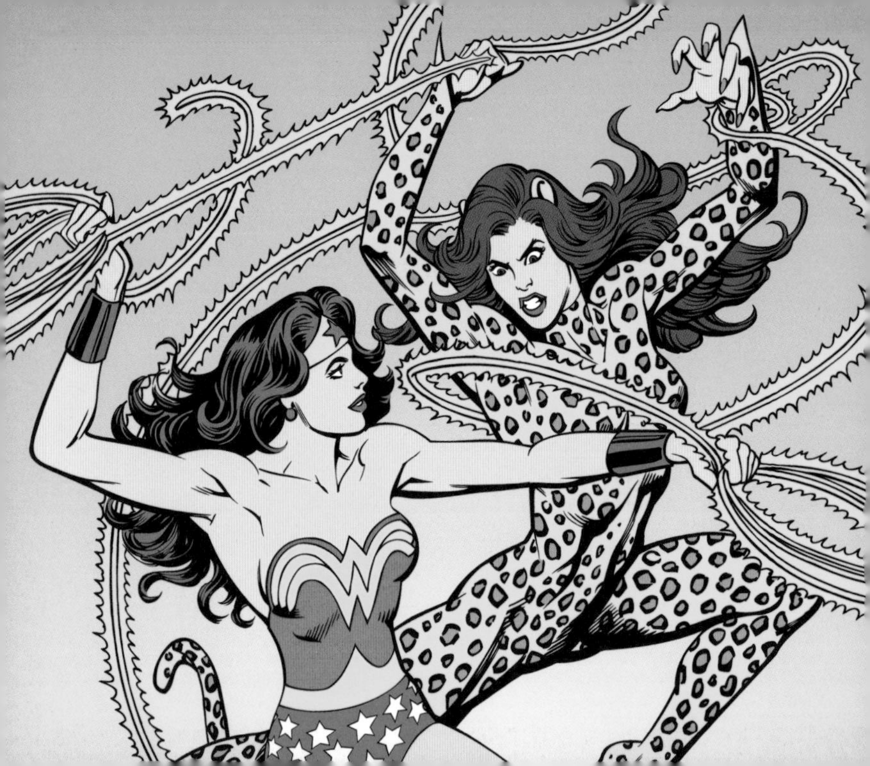

You're heroic because

_____ .

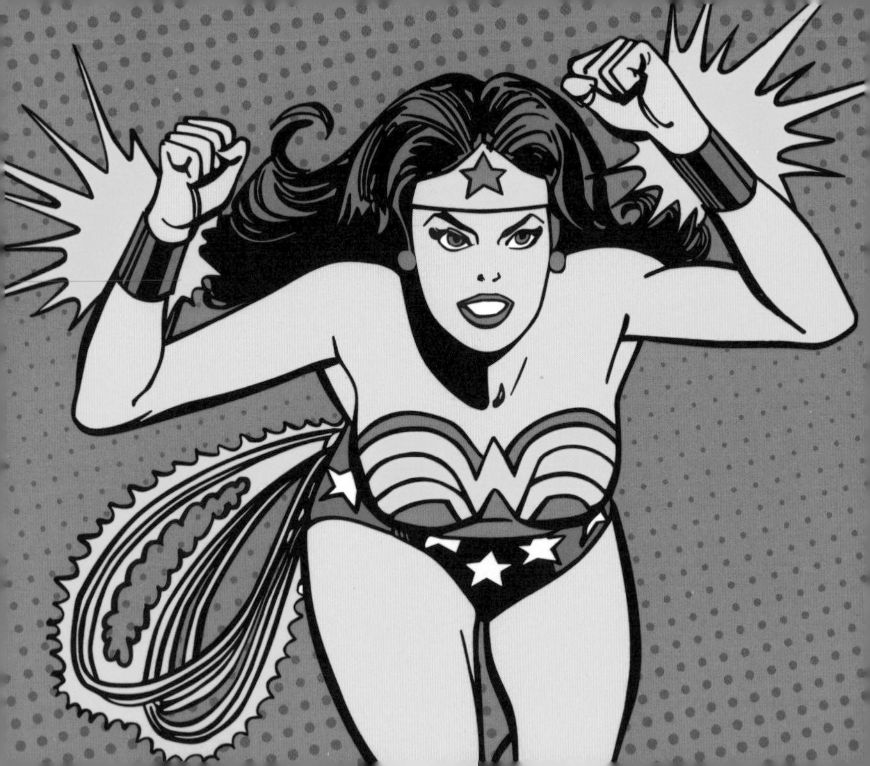

You avoid fights as much
as you can, unless

_____ .

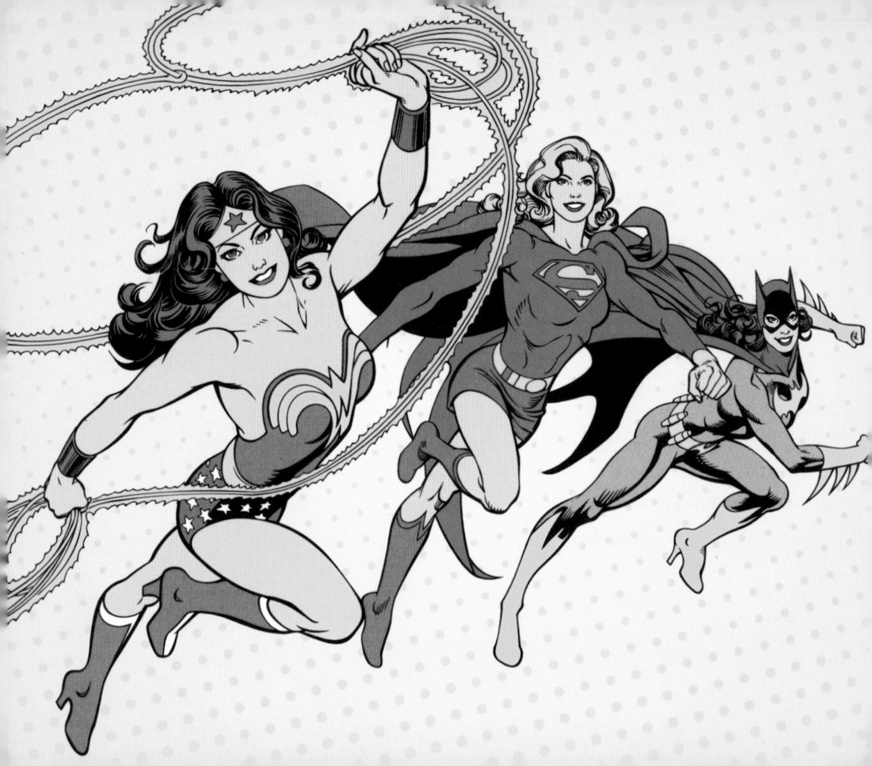

Your sisters look to you for

_____ .

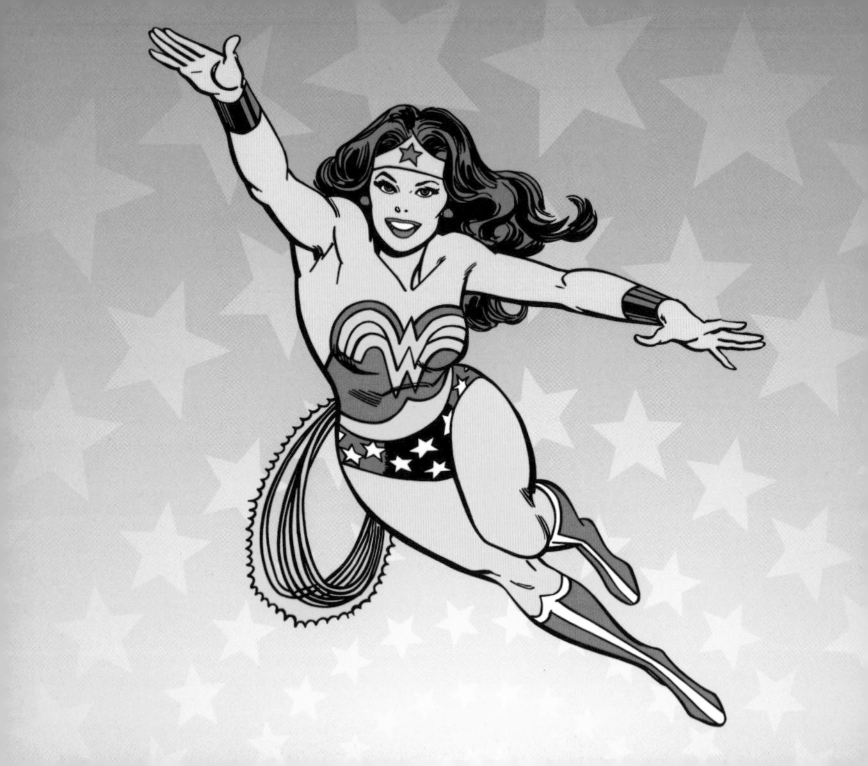

You are as beautiful as Aphrodite,
wise as Athena, stronger than Hercules,
swifter than Mercury, and

_____ .

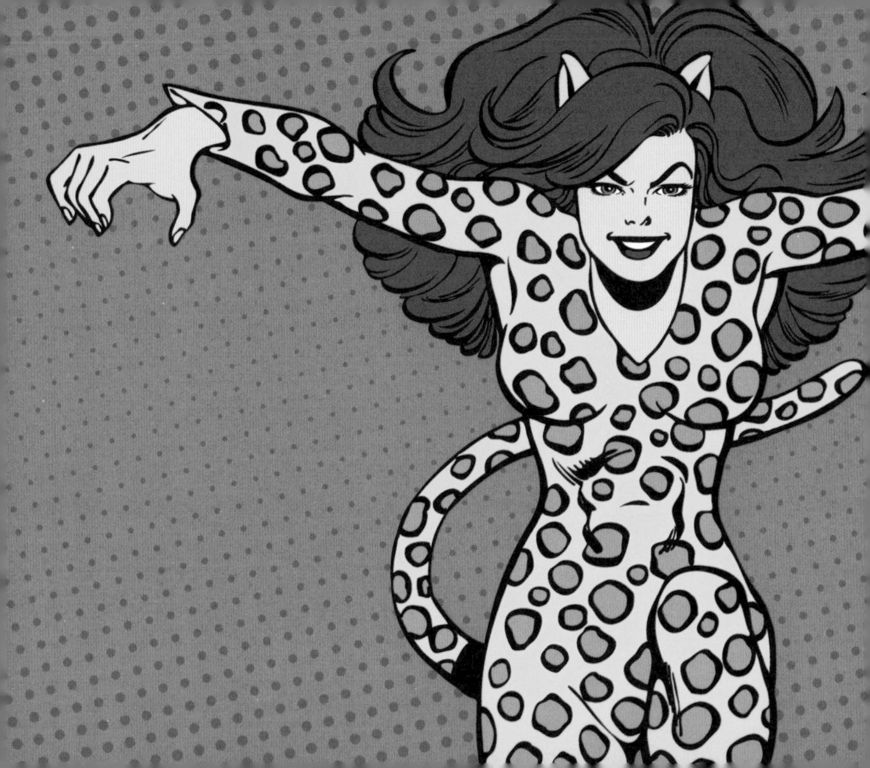

I'm even more jealous of your

_____

than The Cheetah is!

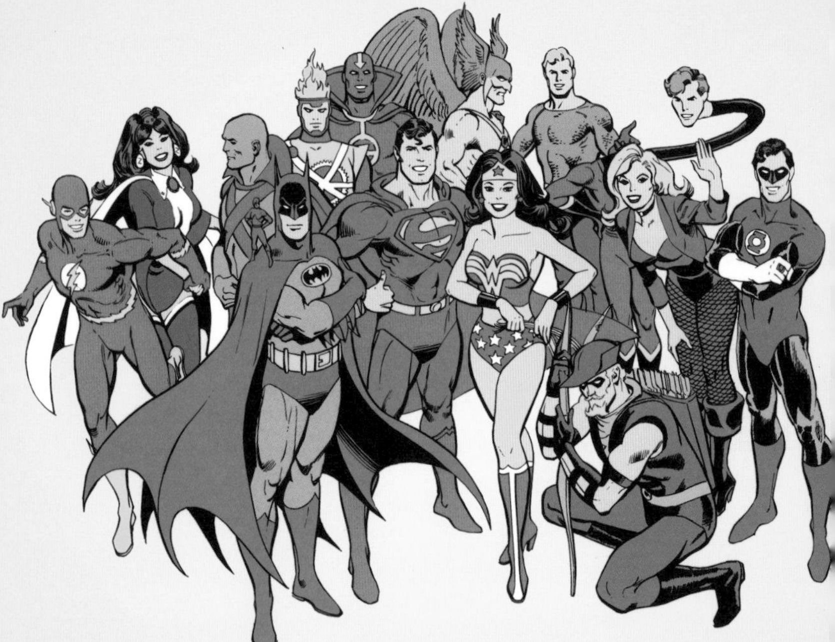

Our super hero team would
be made up of

_____ .

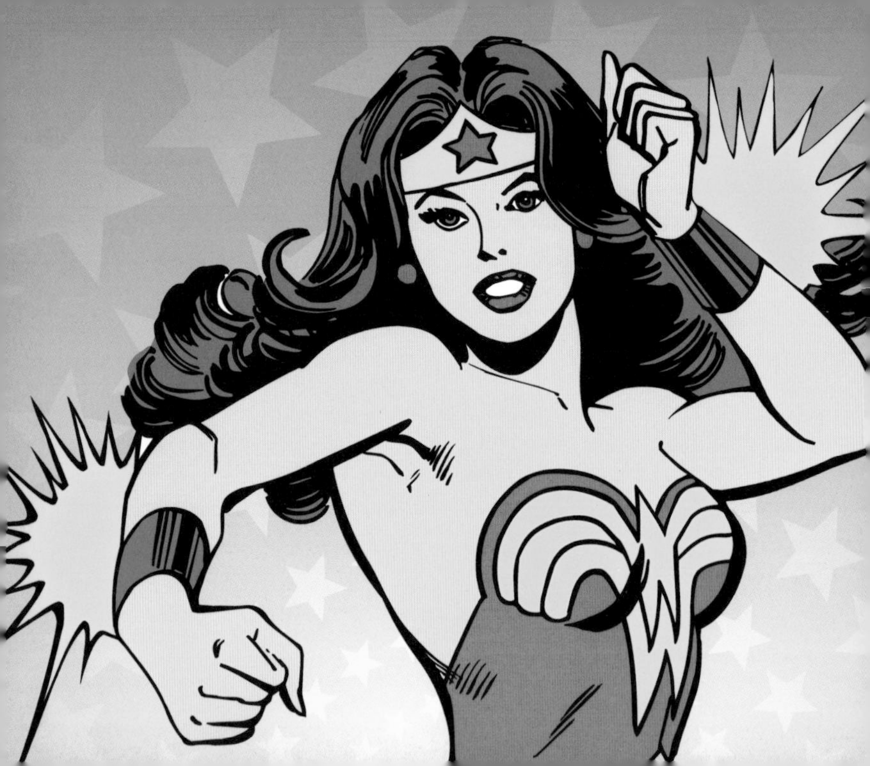

Your theme song would be

_____

sung by

_____ .

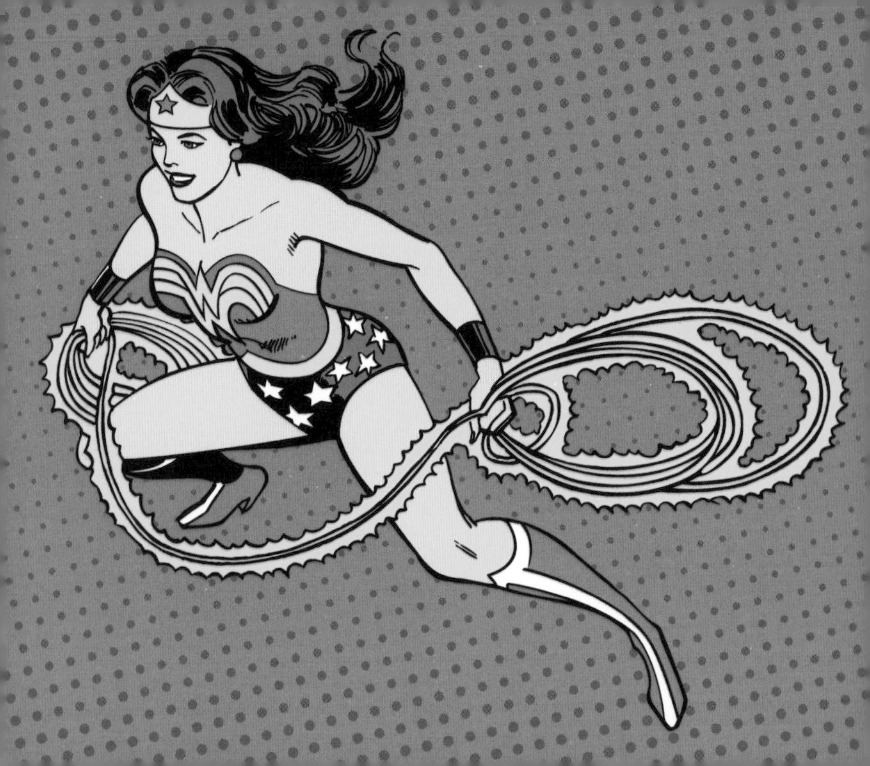

You inspire everyone when you

_____ .

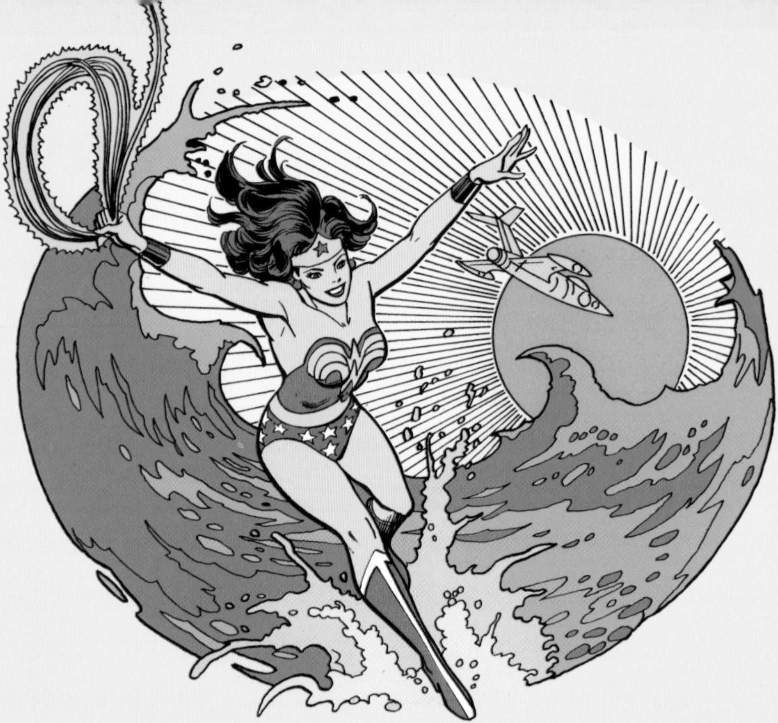

The best part of your origin story involves

_____ .

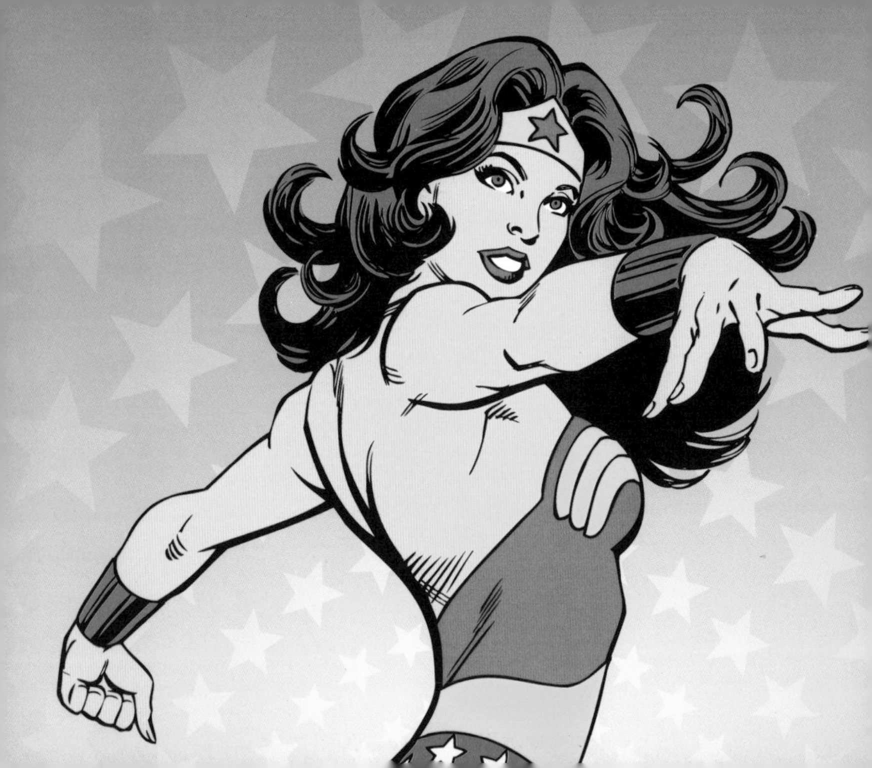

Your determination to

_____

would make Antiope proud.

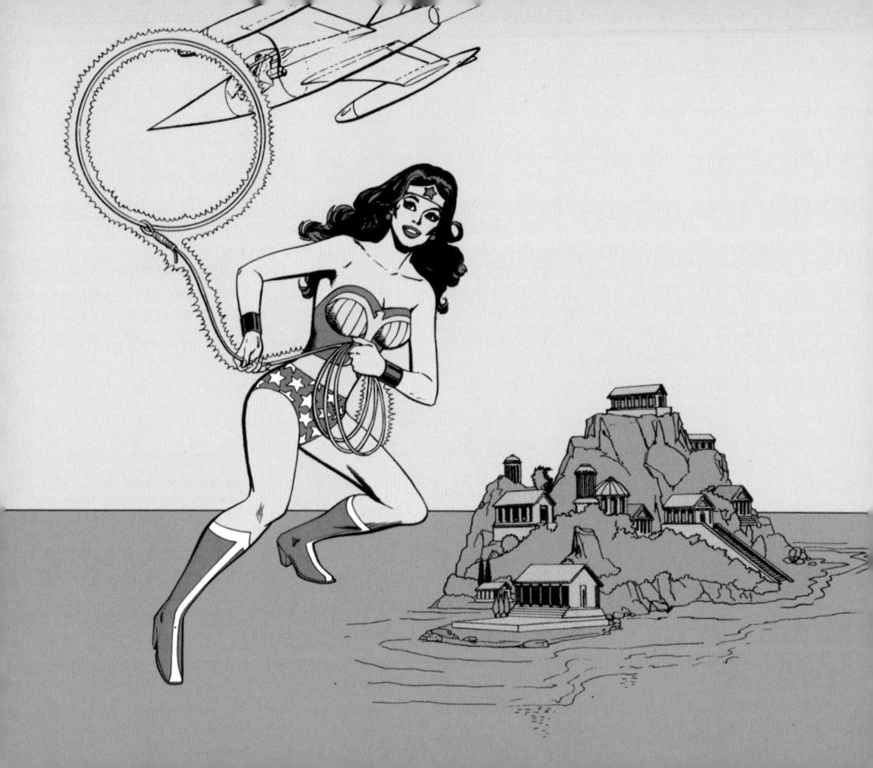

Though you've been everywhere from Themyscira to Paris, your home is wherever

_____ .

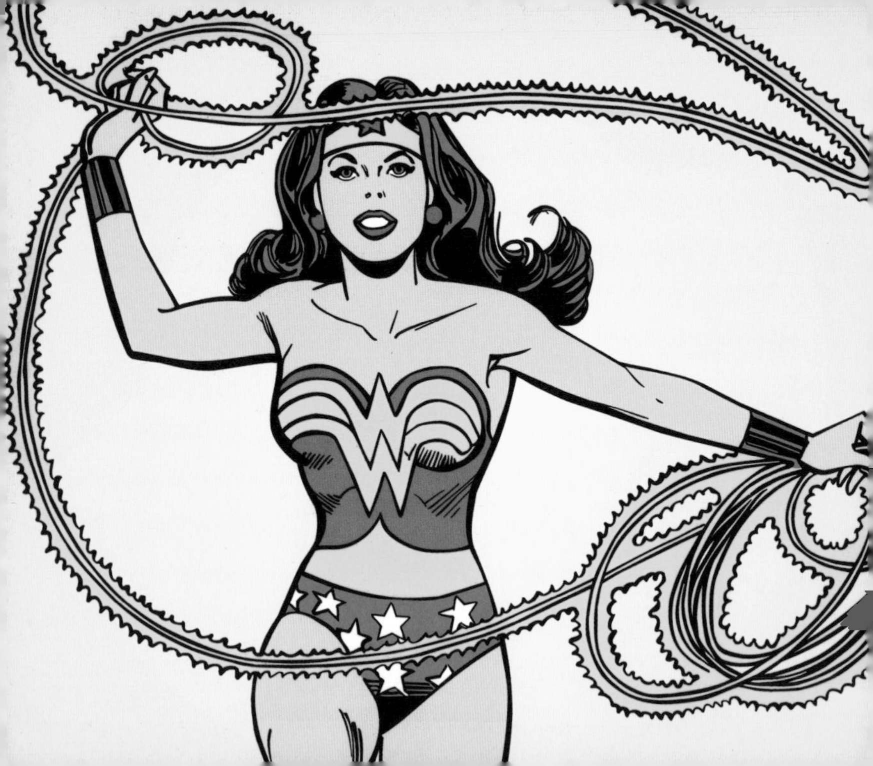

I don't need a magic lasso
to tell you the truth about

_____ .

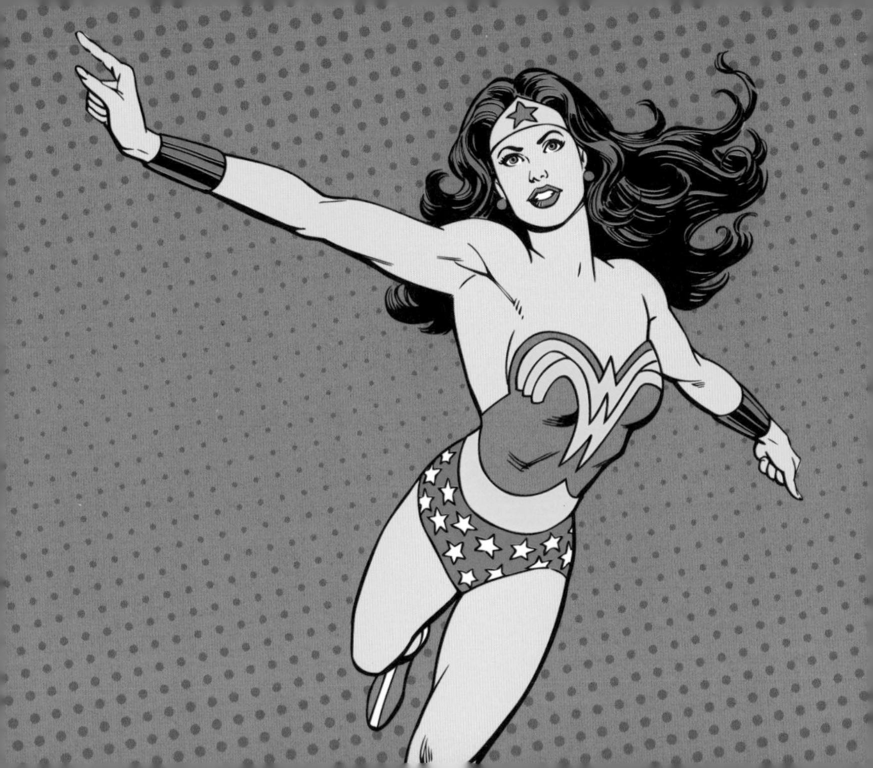

Your faith in

_____

is unshakable.

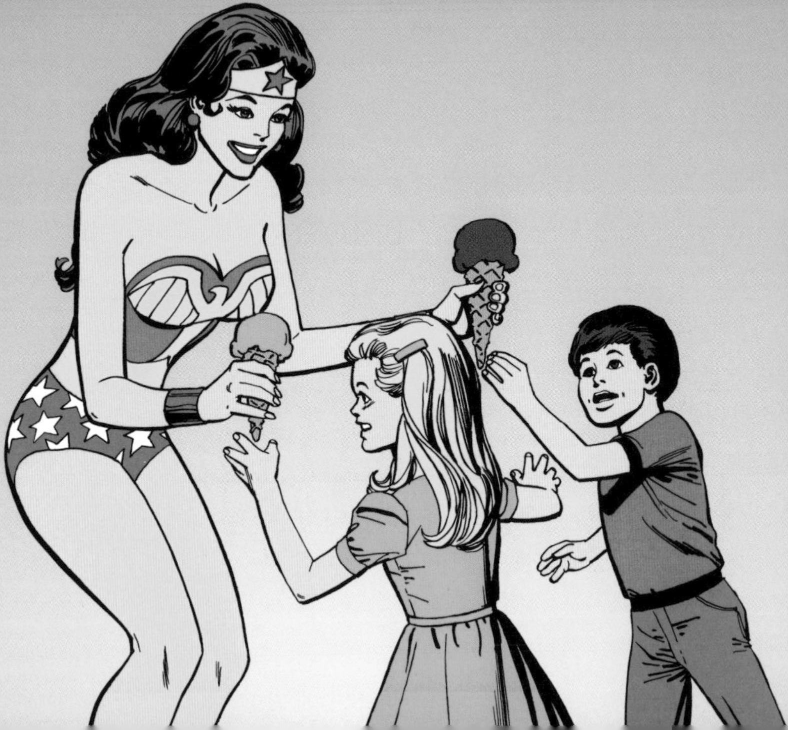

You are devoted to your friends, your

_____ ,

and your family.

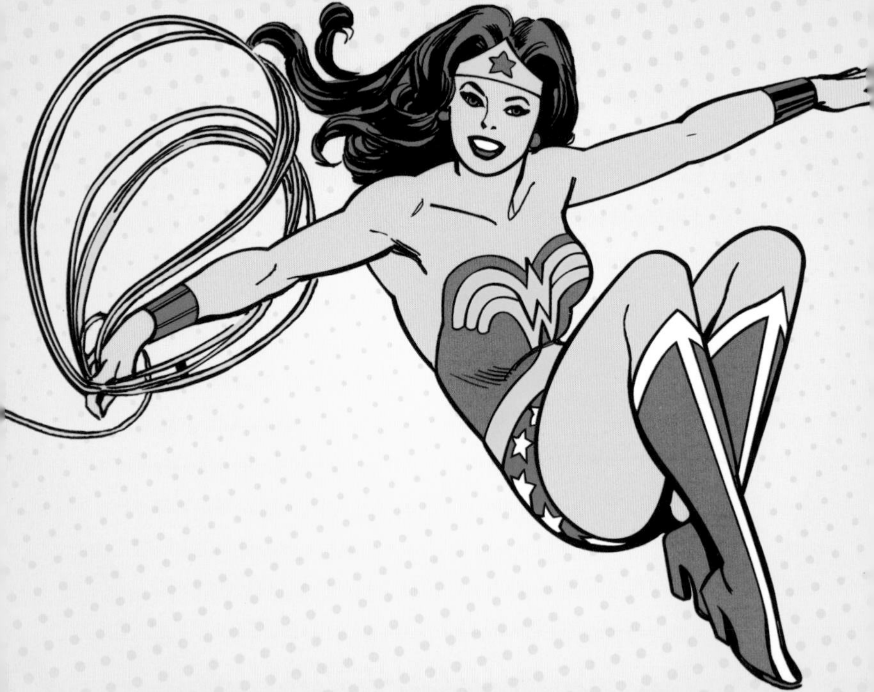

You are destined to

_____.

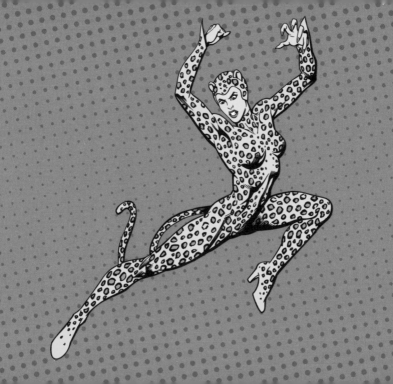

Though it's hard,
you can see the good in anyone,
from The Cheetah to

_____ .

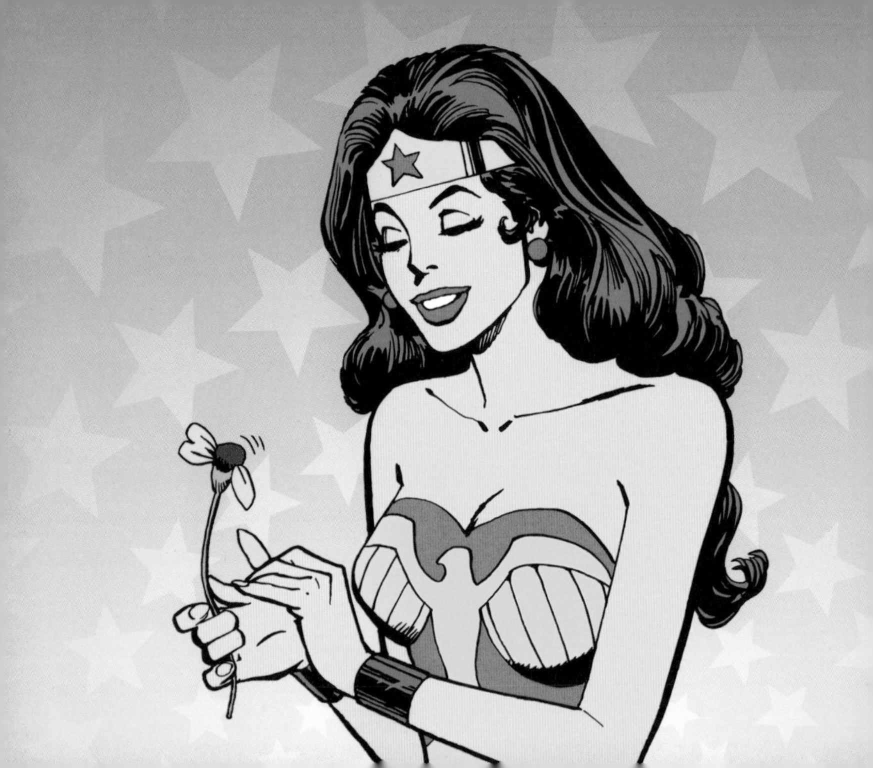

It's not about

_____

for you, it's about love.

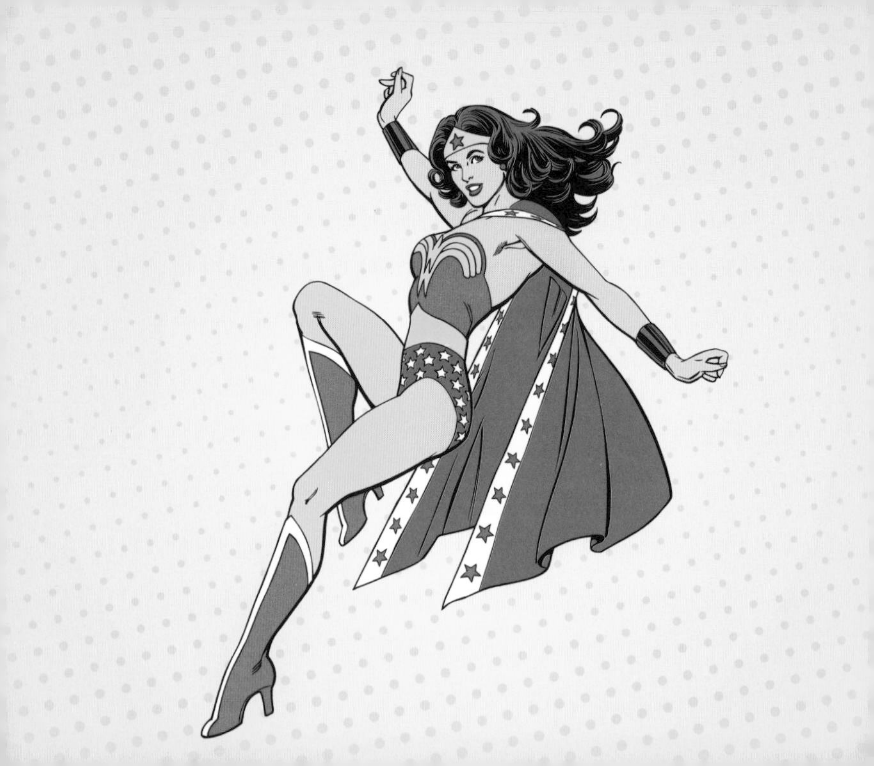

You're wonderful when you

_____ .

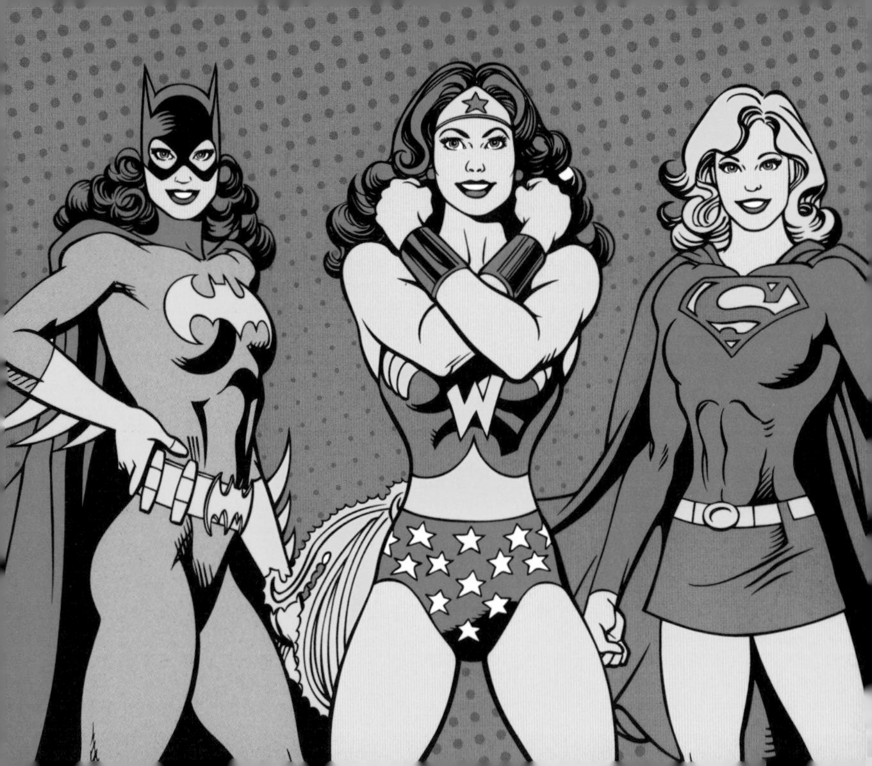

You support your sisters by

_____ .

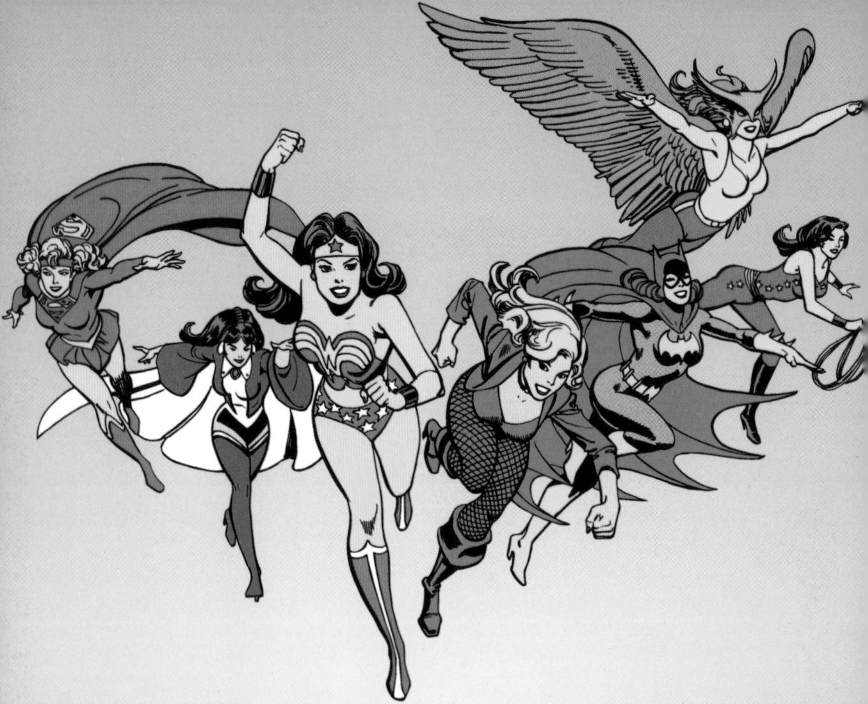

Your sisters will always support you by

_____ .

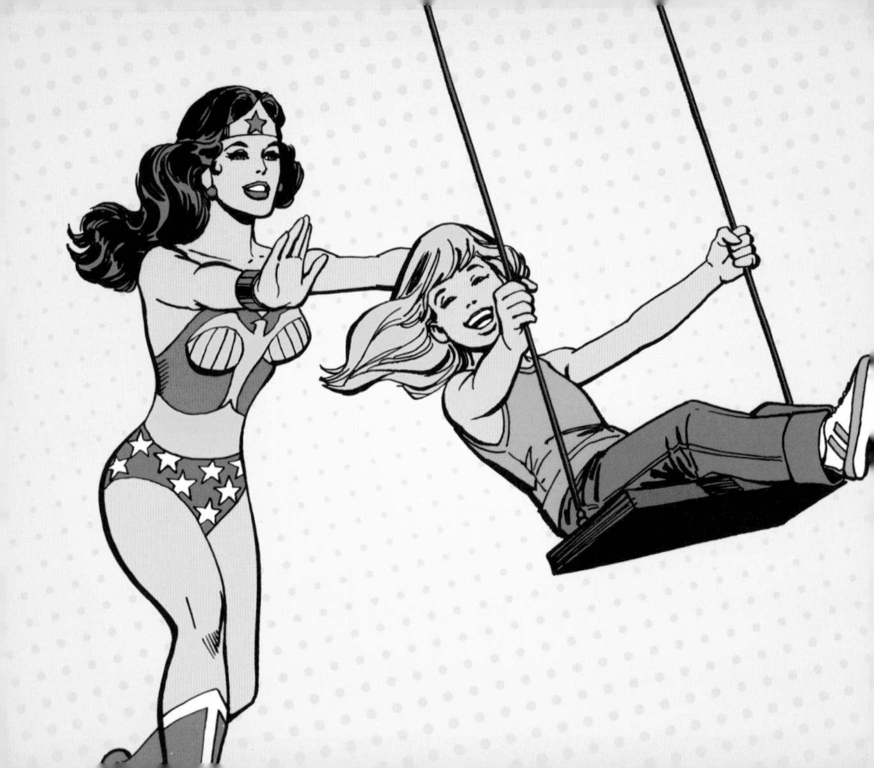

Little girls look up to you because

_____ .

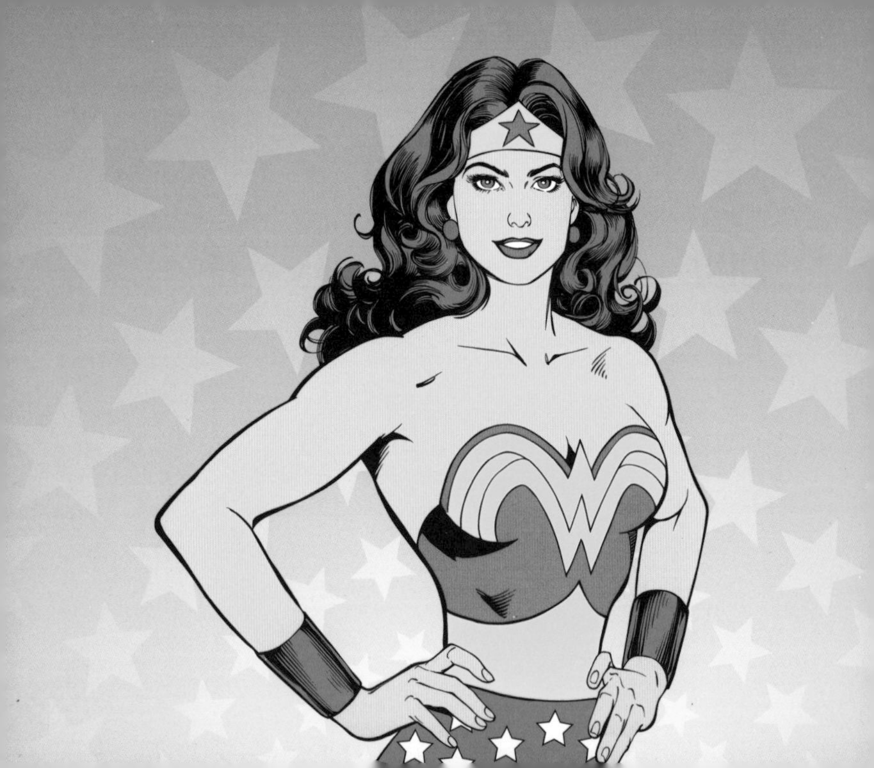

If anyone can pull off wearing

_____

it's you!

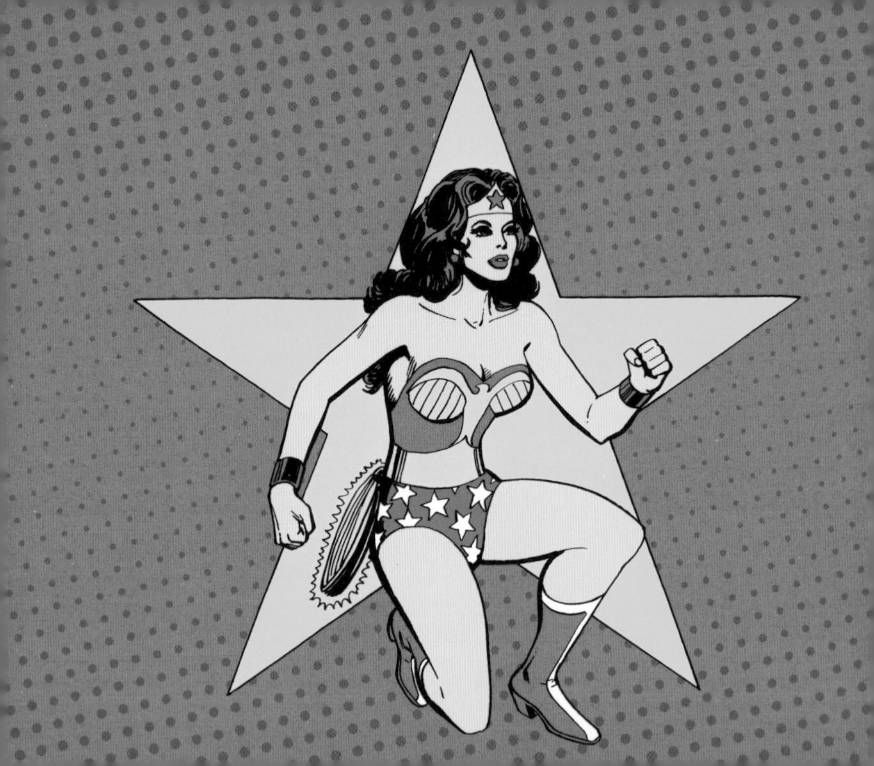

You are a super hero to me.

Hachette Book Group supports the right to free expression and the value of copyright.
The purpose of copyright is to encourage writers and artists to produce the creative works
that enrich our culture.

The scanning, uploading, and distribution of this book without permission is a theft of the
author's intellectual property. If you would like permission to use material from the book
(other than for review purposes), please contact permissions@hbgusa.com. Thank you for
your support of the author's rights.

RP Studio
Hachette Book Group
1290 Avenue of the Americas, New York, NY 10104
www.runningpress.com
@Running_Press

Printed in China
First Edition: April 2019

Published by RP Studio, an imprint of Perseus Books, LLC, a subsidiary of Hachette Book
Group, Inc. The RP Studio name and logo is a trademark of the Hachette Book Group.

The publisher is not responsible for websites (or their content) that are
not owned by the publisher.

Text by Robb Pearlman.
Design by Susan Van Horn.

ISBN: 978-0-7624-6710-5

1010

10 9 8 7 6 5 4 3 2